CAT'S BIRTHDAY DISASTER

by Jenell Boyer

TABLE OF CONTENTS

Chapter One

WHY WEREN'T YOU THERE?

"Where's my new bathing suit? I need it for my big birthday trip this weekend," Cat yelled to her mom across the living room.

"I think it's still in the dryer sweetie," Mom replied.

"But mom, I need to pack all my things for my trip now!" Cat yelled back.

"Honey, you need to wait for it to be done drying. If you use it before it's all the way dry, you could catch a cold," Mom replied.

"Ok," Cat said. "I guess I can wait to pack if I really have to."

Dad came in and asked what we were supposed to be doing right now.

"You know where we're supposed to be! I thought I could trust you Cat," Dad said.

"But dad ..." Cat tried to say, but Dad had already left the room.

"Sweetie, you do know you should have been at that ceremony with your dad. It was a very big deal to him," Mom said.

"Mom, I just had to go to the mall with Stacy and Jamie. They got tickets to the coolest concert in town – Deandra Maybelle!" Cat said.

Mom just sighed and walked away. Cat knew that was her disappointed look. She knew what mom would later say, "Caitlin Elizabeth Johnson, you will be twelve years old this weekend, and you should start acting like it! Just go and do what you are supposed to do sweetheart. It's not hard!"

Cat knew that her mom would tell her to "Do better next time!" And she would try to do better!

Cat (whose actual name is Caitlin) is an obedient tween who just moved to Cabot, Arkansas, from Alamogordo, New Mexico. Mom is the best person to talk to when you need someone to turn to. And dad is a hot-tempered, kind-on-the-inside kind of person. But they make a great family.

Cat had just gone up to her room when the doorbell rang. She ran downstairs to see who it was. When she opened the front door there were two young girls about Cat's age standing there. One had bright blond hair and the other had dark brownish hair. They both looked very friendly. The girl with dark brown hair spoke.

"Hi! My name is Elisa Yang. And this is my twin sister Avery. We were told to bring you and your family these cookies to welcome you to the neighborhood."

"Oh, thank you! I'm Caitlin. But you can call me Cat."

"I was wondering if there was another girl our age living here. How old are you?" Avery asked.

"I'm eleven, I'll be twelve this weekend." Cat replied.

"Oh! That's such a weird coincidence! Our birthday is on Sunday! And we'll be twelve too!" Elisa said.

"Oh wow! My birthday is on Saturday!" Cat said.

"Wow! Do you want to come over and hang out for a bit?" Avery asked. "Come in Avery and Elisa! I'll go ask my mom if I can come over. Most of our stuff is still in the moving van so it's not very furnished yet," Cat said.

"Ok, sounds good!" Elisa said.

"Mom! Can I go over to the neighbor's house, please? They have two girls my age," Cat yelled up the stairs.

"Sure sweetie! Be back by 9:30 tonight. Love you!" Mom yelled.

"Love you too!" Cat yelled back. Then Cat went back into the living room where Elisa and Avery were waiting for her.

"So, what did she say?" Avery asked.

"She said I could come over until nine-thirty tonight!" Cat replied.

"Yay! Alright let's head out then!" Avery said.

About thirty seconds later they arrived at the Yang household. When they walked inside, there were candles burning sweet smelling incense, and there was a huge flat screen on top of a tall tv stand. Then they found the twins' mom on the couch reading a book.

"Hey mom, is it okay to have our new friend Caitlin over?" Elisa asked their mom.

"Sure sweetie. Just try to keep it down because I am in the middle of an interesting book. Ok?" Elisa and Avery's mom said.

"Ok mom! Thanks!" Avery said.

"Oh wait, how long can Caitlin stay?" Elisa and Avery's mom asked.

"Oh yeah, I almost forgot. Sorry mom! She can stay until nine-thirty," Elisa said.

"Ok, thanks sweetie. You can let your friend come up to your rooms now," Elisa and Avery's mom said.

Chapter Two

WANT TO COME ALONG?

Elisa and Avery went back out to the dining room to get Cat.

"Did your mom say I could stay?" Cat asked. "Yes! And I was thinking you might even be able to sleepover tonight if the day goes smoothly," Avery said excitedly.

"That would be so awesome!" Cat replied.

"Hey guys, let's go upstairs now," Elisa said.

The girls quietly went upstairs to Elisa's room.

"Wow!" Cat said when she walked into Elisa's room. "This is such an awesome room! You even have your own flat screen?!"

"Yeah, let's watch a movie! Do you have a favorite?" Elisa asked excitedly.

"Yeah, it's called, "Day in the Life of Samantha Autumn. It's a really good movie." Cat replied.

"Ok, then we'll watch that," Avery said. "Elisa, where's the remote?" she asked.

"It's in the drawer beside my bed." Elisa answered.

"Oh, I found it. Thanks." Avery replied.

After the movie was over, Cat said, "Hey girls, I have a great idea. Do you two want to come with me on my big birthday trip this weekend?" Cat asked.

"Sure! "We can ask our mom if we can go. Are you sure your mom won't mind?" Elisa asked.

"I'm sure she won't mind! She'll probably just be happy that I have some new friends," Cat replied.

"Okay then! When do we leave?" Avery asked.

"Friday morning at four," Cat answered.

"Wait, that's only two days away! Where are we even going?" Elisa asked.

"We're going to Portland, Oregon. We are taking a plane and we're booking tickets tonight. I can ask my mom to book a couple of extra tickets if you girls and your mom want to tag along. The trip is only a week-and-a-half long. And we get to stay at a bunch of different hotels and go to a bunch of cool beaches. And, it can be you girls' birthday trip too since your birthdays are so close to mine!" Cat said.

"I think that sounds like a super great idea!" Avery said.

"Let's go ask mom!" Elisa said.

They the idea to Mrs. Yang and she said that she would give Mrs. Johnson a call to work out the details. "This all sounds like a wonderful idea," said Mrs. Yang. "Thank you for including them Cat! I'm sure we will all have a wonderful time together in Portland."

An hour later, the girls had fallen asleep in Elisa's room while watching a movie. Mrs. Yang called Mrs. Johnson and asked if Cat could sleepover. "Oh yes, that's fine." Mrs. Johnson said.

"Ok, thank you Mrs. Johnson." Mrs. Yang replied.

"No problem! She can come over anytime as long as you guys are around." Cat's mom said.

"Oh, actually the girls wanted me to call you to see if you could book three extra plane tickets to Oregon. Cat wants the girls to come along on her birthday trip this weekend. Elisa and Avery's birthdays are this weekend as well." Mrs. Yang said.

"Oh wow! I wouldn't have guessed they had birthdays in the same month," Mrs. Johnson replied. "And you are welcome to come. I will book three extra plane tickets for Portland."

The next morning Elisa, Avery, and Cat asked Mrs. Yang what Cat's mom had said. "She said that me and the girls can come along on the trip." Mrs. Yang replied.

"Yes!" Cat said. "I'm so excited to have you on the trip!"

"I'm really excited! I'm going to start packing right now." Elisa said.

"Sounds good!" Cat replied.

*

On Friday morning Elisa, Avery, and their mom were at Cat's house. It was three o'clock in the morning. They had all slept over at Cat's house the night before so they wouldn't have to get up quite so early. Everyone was up, showered, packed and ready to leave at four o'clock sharp.

"Dad!" Cat yelled.

"Yes, honey," Cat's dad yelled back.

"Can I please talk to you for a minute?" Cat asked her dad.

"Always, sweetie. Come upstairs so we can talk away from the others." Dad replied. Cat went upstairs and found dad sitting on the upstairs couch ready to talk.

"So, what do you want to talk about, pumpkin?" Dad asked Cat.

"Well, I wanted to talk to you about the little argument we had on Tuesday. I never apologized." Cat said.

"Oh sweetie, I didn't know that the argument made you so upset." Dad said.

"Well, it did. And I just really wanted to

apologize for not being at your promotion ceremony," Cat explained with a frown on her face and eyes beginning to water.

"It's all okay now pumpkin. I know that you 'just had to go' to the coolest concert in town with Stacy and Jamie," Dad replied.

"Well dad, I really just wanted to go because Stacy and Jamie are the only people who are even close to good friends. They are the only new friends I've made since we moved here," Cat said.

"Well next time just tell me that it means so much to you and I will be happy to let you go," Dad replied. "Thanks dad," Cat said. "Now we better get down there or we are going to miss our flight to Portland. We go there every summer on your birthday week and we are not going to stop that tradition now!" Dad said.

So, Cat and her dad went down the stairs and the airport cab picked them up a few minutes later. They all talked and listened to music until they got to the airport.

"I'm so excited Cat!" Avery said.

"Yeah! Thanks for bringing us along Cat! Elisa said.

"I think we are supposed to be at gate eleven by five o'clock. It's already four forty-five. We'd better get a move on." Cat's dad said.

"Hey girls, do you want to come and get a coffee?" Avery and Elisa's mom asked them.

"That's a good idea, Jasmine. It's a long flight to Portland from here." Mrs. Johnson agreed. Just then Cat accidentally knocked over a flight attendant.

"My goodness! I'm so sorry ma'am! Are you okay?" Cat asked her. "Yes, I'm fine, sweetie. What's your name? My name is Kiara Emery." The flight attendant said.

"My name is Caitlin Johnson. I'm terribly sorry for knocking you over." Cat said. "It's alright. You'd be surprised at how many times a week that happens. I am used to it by now," Miss Emery said.

"Ok, I'm sorry to leave you but we should really be going to our gate now. We got here early for a reason." Mrs. Johnson said.

"That's alright dear, I'll be right here when you get back from Portland," said Miss Emery.

"Goodbye now!" Mrs. Yang said.

Chapter Three

WHAT IS IT WITH THAT FLIGHT ATTENDANT?

The next thing they knew, the Yang and Johnson families were on their way to Portland. But nobody had the same suspicions Cat did.

"Mom, did that Miss Emery lady seem a bit suspicious to you?" Cat asked.

"What makes you think she is suspicious Cat?" Mom asked.

"I mean, how could she have known that we were going to Portland?" Cat replied. "Honey, she probably just read our luggage tags," Mom answered.

"I guess," Cat said. But she knew there was something up with Miss Emery.

The flight was going to have a layover in Dallas, Texas. It was about three-and-a-half hours away. Cat had been to Dallas before. But she wasn't staying in Dallas, she was looking forward to spending the entire week in Portland, her hometown. Whenever they visited Portland, they would stay the whole week in their old house that had been turned into a vacation rental a couple years ago. They would also go swimming a lot during the trip. By the time Cat got out of her daydream, Miss Emery was standing over her.

"Hello Cat! Would you like something to drink?" Miss Emery asked.

"Why are you here? And yes, I would like a soda please," Cat replied.

"I had to fill in on this flight for a sick attendant," Miss Emery said.

"Oh, okay," Cat said. Then Miss Emery went over to Cat's mom to say hello. Cat knew they were in big trouble. And since nobody believed that they were in trouble, Cat would have to get to the bottom of it herself.

She watched Miss Emery carefully for the rest of the flight. Then the pilot spoke on the intercom. "Howdy folks! We have reached Dallas, Texas! I hope y'all have enjoyed your flight so far. There will be a bit of landing turbulence as we make our descent. Welcome to Dallas, Texas, everyone!"

Cat and her family got off of the plane to hang out in the airport while they waited for the flight to Portland. "Hey mom, I'm going to go explore this big airport." Cat told her mom.

"No sweetie! You are not wandering around this huge airport by yourself with not even one buddy to protect you! You must take Avery and Elisa with you." Cat's mom said.

"Okay mom. Love you." Cat replied.

"Love you too. Be back here by seven-thirty." Cat's mom said.

"Roger that mom!" And then Cat and Avery left.

"So, what are we really doing?" Elisa asked Cat.

"What do you mean?" Cat replied.

"She means you're acting really weird." Avery said.

"Yeah, you definitely have something on your mind." Elisa agreed.

"What's going on Cat?" Avery asked her.

"Okay guys. I'll tell you what's going on. But you have to promise that you will keep this suspicion a secret from the rest of our families." Cat said.

"Okay, we promise." Avery and Elisa said at the same time.

"Alright then, here goes nothing. You guys remember that lady Miss Emery?" Cat asked them.

"Yes." Elisa and Avery said.

"Well, I think she's up to something that's going to get us all into some real big trouble." Cat said.

"Why do you think that? Elisa asked Cat.

"It's just the way she looked at me. With her fake little smile that stretched out from one cheek to the other," Cat answered.

"Well I guess she is a bit suspicious if you think about it," Avery agreed.

"Yeah, I totally agree with you Cat. She always says hi to the kids and then the adults. Isn't that a bit strange to you?" Elisa asked.

"Yes, it is very strange." Cat answered. "So, I was thinking that me and Avery will follow Miss Emery. Elisa, your job is to find

Miss Emery and then if any trouble comes you go get the parents," Cat told them.

"Got it," Elisa and Avery said.

"Ok, Elisa you go and find Miss Emery and report back here in fifteen minutes. If you are not back by then, we will send the police and our parents to look for you." Cat told Elisa.

"Wait a minute, I didn't know that I might be kidnapped if Miss Emery found out I was looking for her." Elisa said.

"Well, only if Miss Emery was actually bad. Which I think she is actually bad, but I could be wrong. If she finds out you're there, then tell her you got lost and couldn't find your friends."

Cat replied. "Ok I will."

Elisa said. "Good luck!"

Avery and Cat said together. "Thanks! I'll hopefully see you guys soon!" Elisa said.

"We hope so!" Avery and Cat said.

Then Elisa went off to find Miss Emery.

Chapter 4

WHERE ARE YOU ELISA?

It had been fifteen minutes, and there was no sign of Elisa. "Cat, I'm really worried about Elisa. Do you think something bad happened to her?" Avery asked Cat.

"No, she's probably on her way back right now. She probably is worried about worrying us," Cat answered.

"You're probably right Cat. But I am worried," Avery said.

*

Twenty minutes later, Cat regretted telling the parents, but she knew she had to.

She had gotten Elisa into this mess, and she was going to get her out of it. They raced back to the hotel room and told the parents everything as quickly as they could.

"Oh, my goodness! Cat, you sent Elisa out there all by herself just to look for an old lady?" Mom asked her.

"Well, not exactly. We had a plan that once Elisa figured out where Miss Emery was hiding, Avery and I would join her to figure out all the secrets about Miss Emery," Cat explained to her mom, dad, and Mrs. Yang. "I'm so sorry I put your daughter in danger, Mrs. Yang."   The look on Mrs. Yang's face had more worry on it than forgiveness. But Mrs. Yang forced herself to say, "It's alright sweetie, I know you didn't mean to put Elisa in danger."

"Now everyone, what are we just doing sitting here letting poor Elisa suffer out there all alone! Let's go and contact the police, send out an Amber alert, and look for poor Elisa ourselves!" Cat's dad said.

"You're right Mason, we need to go find that poor little girl," Mom told dad.

"Let's hurry! I think I know the direction she went. Miss Emery must have found her and is holding her hostage so that she won't tell what she's doing." Cat said.

"Sweetie, how about I cancel the flight to Portland until we find Elisa," Mom said.

"That would be great, mom. It'll give us more time to look for Elisa." Cat replied.

They went to the police station to file a report, try to get an Amber alert sent out and get more help looking for Elisa.

"I am so glad we found more ways to keep a lookout for Elisa," Mrs. Yang said.

"We will pay every penny to get her back, Jasmine," Mom said.

"Thank you so much," Mrs. Yang said.

Cat, her parents, Avery, and Mrs. Yang spent about five-and-a-half hours looking for Elisa. But by then it was time to eat dinner.

"I know Elisa is important, but we can't look for her on empty stomachs," Cat's dad said. Everyone agreed, so Avery and Cat pointed out a nice little airport restaurant with comfortable looking booths.

"We'd like a table for five, please," Mr. Johnson said.

"Under what name, sir?" the waiter asked Mr. Johnson.

"Please put us under the name Mr. Mason Johnson, thank you." Cat's dad said.

"Okay sir, right this way, if you would," the waiter said. Then, once they were situated in a comfy little booth, a young waitress came over.

"Welcome to 'Marini's House of Pasta and Pizza.' My name is Carol and I will be your waitress tonight," she said.

By the time they got their food, it was already about eight-thirty. Luckily, there was no bedtime when they were on vacation. While they were eating, Cat spotted someone with a kid next to them running across the room. Cat looked closer, and it was Miss Emery and Elisa!

"Mom!" Cat screamed.

"Sweetie, quiet down. What is it?" Mom asked.

"I saw Miss Emery running into the kitchen with Elisa!" Cat said in a rushed voice.

Mrs. Yang heard her too, and she was already running toward the kitchen.

"Mom, dad, run to the kitchen, now!" Cat demanded as she rose from her seat and began running.

Everyone raced into the kitchen. Then Mrs. Yang yelled, "This was all a trick!?"

Chapter 5

WE FOUND HER! NOW WE HAVE ANOTHER PROBLEM...

Everyone had a face that said, "Help me please, I'm confused."

Then Cat explained that Miss Emery and Elisa were just a projection to trick the rest of the Yang and Johnson families.

"They probably just lured us into a trap. We should get out of this kitchen asap!" Cat said. But when they tried to get out of the kitchen, it was locked.

"Cat, Avery, stay close to the adults," Dad whispered. But suddenly, Elisa popped up from one of the countertops all tied up. Well, all except for her mouth.

"Mom, Mr. and Mrs. Johnson, Avery, and Cat? Are you guys just a projection again." Elisa asked cautiously.

"Sweetie, it is really us," Mrs. Yang said.

"Mom don't untie me yet. You could all just get tied up too. This is another trick. I'm real, but nothing else is," Elisa explained.

"Alright sweetie, but how do we get out of here?" Mrs. Yang asked.

"If you untie me from the back you can get us all out of here through the vent safely." Elisa said. "I've known the whole time that I could get out of here, but I've been too afraid to take action myself."

"Okay, we've heard enough from that little blabber mouth of yours, Elisa," a voice said. Then Miss Emery appeared from the newly painted white wall.

"If you want them to be with you so badly, then they'll be with you! All the way to

Paris! Bonjour, Paris!" Miss Emery said with an evil little laugh.

"Have fun!" And then we all dropped down a long, deep, dark hole.

"Mom! Dad!" Cat yelled.

"We're right here sweetie!" both replied.

*

Hours, maybe even a day passed.

"Mom, how long have we been falling?" Cat asked.

"Probably about eleven hours or so," Mom replied. "Where do you think they are sending us to?" Avery asked.

"Remember when Miss Emery said, 'All the way to Paris'? Well, that must be where she is sending us." Mr. Johnson suggested.

"You're right!" Cat said. "But if my theory is correct, there has to be a trap door we can get out of here through. Such a long drop must have access points."

So, everyone started feeling around the walls to see if there was a trap door in there somewhere.

"I think I found an opening!" Elisa said.

"Where?" Cat asked her.

"Right over here." Elisa replied, pointing to a wall on the other side of the big void. Cat felt it to see if it was really an opening that led somewhere other than Paris.

"It is an opening! And by the looks of it, the door opens into Tokyo, Japan!" Cat announced excitedly.

"Ok then, let's get out of this mess!" Mrs. Johnson said. So, they all got out of the void and landed in a delicious smelling restaurant.

"Yum! Something smells delicious!" Avery said. "I think we're in a Japanese restaurant." Cat said.

"Can we get something to eat please mom?" Avery asked her mom.

"Well, I guess a bite to eat wouldn't hurt. What do you think, Abigail?" Mrs. Yang asked mom.

"I think that would be a great idea. And we also need to figure out how to capture Miss Emery so that she doesn't keep trying to harm us," Mrs. Johnson said.

"Yeah, you're right mom. We can't be harmed anymore. I want to get to Portland and have our vacation for all three of our birthdays. My birthday is the day after next, theirs is the day after that, and we're not even in Portland!" Cat said.

"I know sweetie. But we will get to Portland soon enough. For right now we just need to eat and find a nearby hotel." Mrs. Johnson said.

So, they all sat down, ate some noodles and soup, and enjoyed some time relaxing together.

"Mom, how are we going to get to Portland exactly?" Cat asked her. "We will just book a flight to Portland and then go on a plane trip back." Mom told her.

"Or we could go on a cruise back! It could be instead of our birthday trip to Portland!" Cat suggested excitedly.

"Well, that's not a bad idea sweetie. Let us adults talk it over for a little while once we get to the hotel tonight." Mrs. Johnson said.

"Ok mom." Cat said. But inside she was all sorts of excited.

*

That night, while Avery and Elisa were sleeping, Cat crept out of bed quietly to go get a drink. She overheard her mom say, "Well, I don't see why we can't go on a cruise."

Then Mrs. Yang said, "I'm not sure if I can afford a room and all the things we would have to pay for if we went on a cruise."

In her mind, Cat was saying over and over, "Please mom! Just say you can pay for the Yang family!"

Then she heard, "Oh, well I don't see any reason that you guys don't deserve to go on a cruise like us. We'll pay for you guys to come with us on the cruise."

"Thank you, Abigail. This means a lot," Mrs. Yang replied.

"Don't mention it!" Mom said.

*

The next morning, the Johnson and Yang families checked out of the hotel and were on a flight to a place a couple hundred miles away from Tokyo.

"So, who thinks a cruise would be a good idea for a vacation instead of Portland this year?" Mom asked everyone.

Chapter 6

HOW DID WE GET HERE?

"I do!" everyone answered at the same time.

"Ok, then! Mrs. Yang and I have decided to let you girls stay in your own room." Mom said.

"But you have to promise us that you'll never leave the room without one of the adults' permission. Ok?" Mrs. Yang told the girls.

"Ok!" Cat, Elisa, and Avery said.

Then the flight attendant spoke over the intercom, "We are going to be experiencing a bit of turbulence as we make our descent into Hahohi, Japan."

So, everyone held on to each other, worried that this might be another setup to hurt the families. Fortunately, the plane landed safely within half an hour.

"I'll go grab our bags downstairs. You girls stay safe and keep an eye out for Miss Emery!" Dad said.

"Ok, dad! We will sure try not to get kidnapped again!" Cat said.

*

An hour later, everyone was waiting at the docks for the cruise ship to arrive.

"Mom! When will the ship be here? It's taking forever!" Cat complained to her mom.

"Sweetie, I've told you a hundred times! It will get here within an hour or so!" Mom replied, with a touch of frustration in her voice.

Just then, the ship that they were supposed to get on pulled up to one of the docks. "Wow! It's so big! Let's go!" Avery yelled over all the noise of passengers boarding.

"Okay, honey," Mrs. Yang said.

So, they all got on the ship and settled into their bedrooms.

"Okay girls, you behave yourselves in here. And don't order too much from the room service menu. I don't want you to get sick," Mom said.

"We'll be fine, mom! I promise we won't order anything more than three meals a day and three snacks," Cat said. Avery and Elisa nodded in agreement.

"Ok, then. Love you! We will see you tomorrow morning on the deck for breakfast!" Mom replied.

The adults left the room and went down the hall to their room. "We're free!" The three girls said all at once.

"Let's order a snack now!" Elisa suggested. The others thought it was a great idea, so they looked over the room service snack menu.

"How about cheese and guacamole dip with tortilla chips?" Avery asked.

"Yes! That sounds absolutely delicious!" Elisa and Cat agreed.

*

An hour later their food arrived. The plate was absolutely gigantic! "Where do we start?" Cat asked.

"I don't know!" Avery said.

"I do, let's dig in and stuff our faces!" Elisa said.

"Now that's a plan!" Cat agreed. So, the girls stayed up late ordering more and more food, and watching movies and hanging out on the balcony.

"This is the best trip ever!" Elisa said. Then Cat said, "Tomorrow, it'll be even better! We get to go swimming in the big pool that has twenty-two different swirly slides!"

"Yeah, but I can't help wondering why Miss Emery kidnapped me in the first place," Elisa said.

"She probably took you because you won the science fair, and you've already received a letter from the high school back at home offering for you to go there early!" Avery said.

"Seriously?" Cat asked.

"Seriously!" Avery replied.

"Well, I don't want to brag." Elisa said.

"Wow," Cat replied. I wonder why Miss Emery would need to use your brilliant mind. She's probably got a super evil plan stirring up in that NOT-SO-SMART little brain of hers."

"Hey guys, check it out!" Elisa pointed to their ship's schedule. "It looks like we found just who we need to." She said. They all looked at the program and saw who their captain was, Captain Kiara Emery.

Chapter 7

THE RISE AND FALL OF THE MISS EMERY EMPIRE

"How could Miss Emery possibly be a flight attendant and a captain?" Cat asked her friends.

"Well, I just searched up 'Kiara Emery' on the internet and it says she's a disgrace to the law, a kidnapper, and almost every person she encounters fears for their safety. I guess nobody here in Japan knows she's on the other side. She's bad." Elisa told them.

"Well I guess we need to go try to find out what she's up to," Avery said.

"I agree with Avery. We need to figure out what's going on here. We could all be in huge danger," Cat said.

"Ok then, what do you say Elisa?" Avery asked.

"I say it's a great idea." Elisa agreed.

"Then what are we waiting for? Let's go!" Cat said.

*

They reached the Captain's Lounge a few minutes later and decided they should not split up. "We need to stick together if we don't want to get caught." Cat whispered to the others.

"You're right Cat. Come on in girls, I have a plan." Elisa said, taking control.

The girls went inside the lounge and ducked under a big potted plant.

"There she is." Avery said, pointing at Miss Emery.

They listened to Miss Emery talking to someone else in the seat beside her, "Oh, Susan, when will I finally find someone clever enough to bring back my Thomas? I miss him so much every time I think about him."

"Well Kiara, you didn't have to let go of that ridiculously smart girl, Elisa Yang. I hear she got an offer to go to high school when she's only going into the sixth grade," Susan replied. "I didn't let go of her, she got away with the rest of those filthy brats who don't want me to ever be happy." Miss Emery said.

"Well, I bet you a million that if you had kept that Elisa girl you would've had your Thomas back by now." Susan replied.

"That's why I'm pretending to be captain of this ship, because I looked at the passenger list and found out that all those filthy brats are on this ship on a 'family vacation' for the week." Miss Emery said.

"Well, they probably don't realize why you want to take Elisa. If they knew, I'm sure they would've let you borrow Elisa for an afternoon to figure out how to get the love of your life back," Susan said.

*

After that, the girls started back to their room. When they got there, they decided what they had to do to save everyone – they had to let Miss Emery kidnap Elisa.

"I think she would definitely let me go after I help her get 'the love of her life' back. All I have to do is build a time machine and take her back to save 'her Thomas.' It's simple," Elisa told them.

"Okay then, it's settled, Elisa is getting kidnapped tomorrow," Cat said.

Avery nodded, so they knew it was time to take their plan into action.

*

Before they knew it, the girls were all sneaking up the steps to the Captain's Lounge.

"You remember what to say, right Elisa?" Avery asked her sister.

"Yes, I'll be fine, don't worry," Elisa replied.

"Okay then, you'd better be off. Good luck!" Cat and Avery called after her.

And with that, Elisa went inside the captain's lounge, not knowing what would happen next.

To be continued ...

9 7 9 8 6 1 0 2 0 7 9 0 2